D0575050

For Jack

ISBN 0-8109-3740-9

First published in Great Britain in 1995 by
National Trust (Enterprises) Ltd., London

Published in 1995 by Harry N. Abrams, Incorporated, New York
A Times Mirror Company

Designed by Butterworth Design
Production by Bob Towell

Printed and bound in Hong Kong

Ian Penney's ~ Book of ~ Fairy Tales

Illustrated by Ian Penney

Harry N. Abrams, Inc., Publishers

This book belongs to

....

Contents

The Princess and the Pea

Long ago, in a part of England called the Shire of Derby, there was a very unhappy Prince, living in a very beautiful house called Kedleston. He wasn't unhappy because he was lonely, or because he didn't want to be a prince – he had lots of friends and being a prince seemed to him to be pretty good fun. He was unhappy because his parents wanted him to find a princess and, despite searching high and low throughout the shire, he could not find a single one he liked enough to marry – or not a real one anyway.

"Maybe you need to try a bit further afield," said his father one day, when the Prince was looking particularly glum. "There are lots of other parts of the country, a long way from Kedleston, where you could search for a real princess. Why don't you go off on a trip?"

"Do I really have to?" asked the Prince, "Can't I stay just as I am? I don't really want to go off travelling, and I'll only get everyone's hopes up – they'll see me coming and go to all sorts of lengths to try and persuade me to marry them just because I'm a prince. Couldn't I just wait for the right person to come along?"

"Absolutely not," said his father, "I had to hunt everywhere for your mother – took me years to find her! And besides, you'll only get up to all sorts of trouble hanging around here! You had better get going – Kedleston needs a princess and you need a wife!"

So the Prince set off on a tour to find one. He visited all the beautiful castles and palaces that he could find, from the Welsh mountains to the Norfolk countryside, from the Northumbrian hills to the South Downs, and found hundreds of princesses, all wearing magnificent dresses and covered in dazzling jewels – but none of them seemed to have quite enough . . . well, quite enough *princessness* about them.

"What on earth do you mean?" said his parents when he returned empty handed, "Why aren't they good enough for you? Some of them must be beautiful, or rich or talented – or all three! What does it matter if they are not *quite* royal enough?"

"Anyway," said the Queen, "you can always tell a *real* princess." "How?" asked her son. "Never you mind," said the Queen, "One day, when it really matters, you will find out." The Prince did not question her any further – his mother had lots of funny old ideas about royalty that all seemed a bit like hocus pocus to him. *He* was a modern prince, and didn't believe in such things. "I give up," thought the Prince sadly, as he slouched off to his room. His parents had no choice but to try to cheer him up as best they could until he found a real princess to marry.

One night, not long after this, everyone in the palace was asleep when a terrible storm began to rage. Thick sheets of rain began to fall, a wild wind lashed around the palace with an almighty howl, and tremendous thunder and lightning made

everyone tremble beneath their eiderdowns and feel thankful that they were safe inside. In the middle of all this, the King heard the bell ring at the palace door. It kept on ringing, until the King decided he would have to answer it himself. "Useless staff," he muttered as he put on his dressing-gown and clomped downstairs in his slippers to answer the door. "No decent princesses to be found, no decent servants to be had – what *is* the world coming to?"

He hauled the door open and rain began to sweep into the palace. The King quickly tried to heave the heavy old door shut, when he realised that a young woman had also been swept in by the raging storm, and lay exhausted at his feet. He bent to pick her up and found that she was pale and shivering and completely wet through. Her hair was plastered in rats' tails around her head and her bedraggled clothes were soaked through. Astonished by the vision of this pitiful creature, he asked who she was. "I'm a Pppppprincess," she said, through chattering teeth, "A rrrrreal one."

Everyone in the palace was now wide awake, including the Queen who was demanding to know what was going on. When the King explained that he had opened the door to a real princess, his wife looked very doubtful. "Oh yes?" she said to herself, "Let's see if you really are what you say." So she went into the spare bedchamber and started to prepare the spare royal bed. She took off the mattress and placed a tiny, wrinkled, dried pea in the middle of the bed. Then she added, not only one mattress, but fifteen more that she gathered from all the beds around the palace, having thrown all the other minor royalty in the palace out of their beds for the night. And on top of these she placed fifteen royal eiderdowns.

"Now let's see who's really royal," she said, chuckling merrily and rubbing her hands together. "Come my dear," she called to the new guest, "let's put you to bed for a good night's rest. I've prepared the most splendid and comfortable bed

in the whole palace for you." And she sat the Princess down before the royal fire to warm up, gave her a royal silk nightgown and a special mug of royal milk and honey, and then packed her off to bed, up a little royal step-ladder, to the top of the pile of mattresses and eiderdowns.

After the Princess had gone to sleep, the Queen called her husband and son together and told them about her little test. "The proof is in the pea my dears – if she feels that tiny pea under all that padding then she is a princess beyond all doubt!" The Prince sighed in disbelief but decided he had nothing to lose by waiting to see if his mother was right.

The next morning the Princess came downstairs looking even more pale and exhausted. "Oh it was awful," she cried. "I felt that I was sleeping upon a horrid rock – goodness knows what was in the bed! There might as well have been no mattresses there at all for all the comfort I got!" The Princess had felt the pea under all those mattresses! The King and Queen immediately clapped their hands together with joy, while their son almost choked on his porridge in amazement – for they all knew that only a real princess could possibly have such delicate and sensitive skin.

So the Prince and Princess were married, all the other beds got their mattresses back, and the pea was removed from their beautiful bed and kept safely in a glass case – just in case they ever needed to test anyone else out in the future. And the Prince never doubted the Queen's funny old ideas again.

The Willow Plate Story

People who lived in grand houses over two hundred years ago often went on long journeys around the world, collecting works of art and ornaments on their travels. Because of this, many houses are filled with all sorts of treasures from Europe, India, or China. Porcelain from China was so popular in Europe that English pottery makers copied Chinese designs onto their own plates and cups, or made up their own designs in the Chinese style. Sometimes these designs showed more than just pretty pictures – they told a story . . . .

A young Chinese girl lived with her father in an old Chinese pagoda, and in front of the pagoda was a huge old weeping willow tree. Its branches swept down into the clear blue waters of an ancient river, which carried ships out to the High China Seas and, in the autumn, the willow's fallen leaves formed a soft, moving carpet upon the water. Wonderful flowers surrounded the pagoda, and filled its rooms with magical fragrances.

But her world was not always a happy one. Her garden was surrounded by a high bamboo fence and she was forbidden ever to go beyond it. When she was little, her father, an old Chinese mandarin, had promised her hand in marriage to an old merchant, and he would not allow her to talk to anyone else before her wedding day.

The mandarin's daughter had to be content with the fish in the river and the swallows in the sky as her friends. She talked to them of her hopes and fears, and fed them grains of rice from her hands.

But she did not go unseen. One of her father's servants looked after the beautiful gardens and he, too, came to know all the fish and the birds. Most days he would stand on the little bridge across the river and watch the mandarin's daughter feed his little friends from her window. Finally she began to notice the young man on the bridge, and one day she sent a message to him, carried in the beak of one of the swallows. He replied immediately, and they began to correspond in this way every day. It was not long before the servant suggested that they meet, at the next full moon, on the banks of the river.

When the full moon came, the mandarin's daughter crept out of the pagoda and under the willow tree, where the long branches hid her from sight. There the couple were united at last – but she had been followed. No sooner had they spoken than her furious father swept back the branches, and banished the young man forever. His daughter wept many tears for her lost love, and declared she would not marry the old merchant. So her father locked her away in a house on an island in the middle of the ancient river.

The day of her wedding finally arrived, but the mandarin's daughter did not believe her beloved would let the marriage take place – and she was right. Before the vows were spoken, he appeared, disguised as a river boatman, and pulled her from the altar. The two took flight across the bridge, with the bride's father in pursuit. When he failed to catch them, he sent his servants in search of them, and the servants used the devoted swallows to guide them to the couple.

When they were finally captured, the mandarin locked them up on the island, with no food and water, and they died in each other's arms, in a room looking out over the ancient river and the weeping willow.

But their story does not quite end there. The gods took pity on the poor lovers and turned them into a pair of swallows. The birds immediately flew up high into the sky above the pagoda. And there they remain today; above the willow tree, in a Chinese landscape, on the blue and white plate, in countless houses around the world. So if you ever see one of these blue and white willow pattern plates, look closely at the sad story that it tells. And if you look at the plate for long enough, you could be forgiven for thinking that the people and the birds in the blue and white world are almost real . . . .

Rapunzel

There was once a very beautiful tower, in the heart of a garden called Trelissick, on the coast in Cornwall. The garden was full of rare plants and flowers, and there were wonderful woodland walks which ran beside open fields, and a river which ran down to the sea. The tower provided stunning views over the estuary and the harbour below, and most afternoons, sailors coming into harbour could see a beautiful young woman staring out to sea from the top of the tower. The beautiful woman was called Rapunzel.

Rapunzel had long, golden hair which she wore in a long braid. Rapunzel had a very sunny nature, but had lived most of her life under very cruel circumstances. As a baby, she had been snatched from her parents by an evil Cornish witch, who had imprisoned her in Trelissick Tower. The tower had neither a staircase nor a door – only tiny little windows high up in the roof.

Whenever the witch wanted to gain access to the tower, she stood at the bottom and called, "Rapunzel, Rapunzel, let down your hair." Then Rapunzel would let down her long golden braid and the witch could climb up and enter the tower through the little window.

Despite the beautiful views and her wonderful setting, Rapunzel was very lonely in her tower, and she tried to find ways to pass the time. She would paint the view from her window over and over again until she had created hundreds of images of the Cornish sea in all weathers. She would spin wool which she could never knit into anything as the witch would not permit her to have any knitting needles, and when these pursuits began to bore her, she learnt to sing. She only knew one very sad song which she sang every morning to a plaintive, ancient melody as she beckoned the birds to her window:

"Come to me, come to me
Jackdaws and swallows,
As you swoop up into the blue.
You know nothing of all my endless sorrows
Or how I long to be free like you."

The sailors below would hear this lament as they set out to sea, and pity the beautiful young woman alone in her tower. One day, a young Cornish prince rode by Trelissick and heard Rapunzel's sweet, sad song echo through the garden. Stunned by her beautiful voice, he made up his mind to meet its mysterious owner, but he could see no way of reaching her. He returned to the tower that very evening and, as the light faded, he saw a wizened old witch approach. He hid behind a magnificent rhododendron bush and heard her call out, "Rapunzel, Rapunzel, let down your hair."

W
N
S
E

Then he watched in amazement as Rapunzel's hair descended from the window, and the witch climbed up.

The next day, he came to the tower a little earlier, and called softly, "Rapunzel, Rapunzel, let down your hair." Down came the loosened braid, and the Prince climbed up it, into Rapunzel's room. He found himself falling through the window onto a pile of her paintings and a mound of freshly spun balls of wool. The terrified Rapunzel was soon won over by his gentle manner, as the Prince declared his intention of removing her from her prison. But as he climbed down from the tower, he failed to see the witch watching him from the woods.

He returned the next day, bringing with him a long rope borrowed from one of the fishing boats, but when he got to the top of the tower, he found that the braid had been cut from Rapunzel's head, and was held by the old witch. "I have banished the girl into the woods where you will never find her," she cried. And she ran at him, pushing him from the window and onto a thorn bush below, where the bush's jagged thorns blinded him as he stumbled.

The blind Prince spent many days wandering the coast in search of Rapunzel, hoping that somehow he would find her. He was resting one day at a little cove near Trelissick, when he heard her beautiful voice – distant but unmistakable – calling to the birds. He called out in response, and when she found him, her tears of happiness fell into his wounded eyes, restoring his sight. She vowed then that she would never grow her hair again – and that she would live on the ground floor in future, away from the sea view and the birds that she had grown up with, and close to the Cornish earth that she had never been able to touch.

The Legend of Finn McCool

Many years ago, there lived an Irish giant called Finn McCool. He was absolutely *enormous*, and had tremendous difficulty finding any clothes to fit him. He had to get special outfits made by having lots of blankets stitched together by the only tailor in Country Antrim who wasn't afraid of him. Finn was married to a giant called Oonagh, and they had a baby son called Oisin. Even Oisin's tiny steps could make the ground tremble, and Finn's thunderous voice could be heard for miles around.

Finn and his family lived on a spectacular bay called Port Noffer. One night they were woken by a hideous screeching noise coming from over the water – a giant called Benandonner lived across the sea in Scotland, and he was playing the bagpipes so loudly that they kept Finn's family awake all night.

The following night, Finn, already irritable, was woken by the same ghastly noise, coming all the way across the sea to North Antrim. Benandonner had recently taken up the bagpipes in an effort to cure his insomnia – giants sometimes have great difficulty sleeping, as it is almost impossible to get comfortable when no bed is big enough for you. Benandonner wasn't very good at playing the bagpipes as he still had a lot to learn, but Finn decided that he wasn't going to give Benandonner the chance to practise any more.

Finn's favourite hobby was carving different shapes from the wood and the basalt (a type of rock) which he found on his beach. As he sat carving and listening to the wailing from across the waters, an excellent idea occurred to him. He made up his mind to build a causeway across the sea in order to fight the Scottish giant. He set about carving lots of huge stepping stones in different sizes, and six-sided, to place in the sea all the way to Scotland. When he had finished this huge task he loaded all the stones onto his back and set off, throwing them in front of him as he went. "Fe, fi, fo, fum," he cried as he went, "I'll stop the tune of the bagpipe man!"

He arrived on Scottish land, on the Isle of Staffa, in the middle of the night but couldn't find Benandonner anywhere, so he had to wait until daylight when he could search along all the beaches and behind all the hills. Eventually, as morning broke, he heard the familiar dreadful wailing coming from over the mountains, and Finn set off to find the Scottish giant. Unfortunately for Finn, he had never seen his

rival except at a huge distance. Benandonner was not only much taller than Finn, but looked much more ferocious. He was a West Highland giant: he wore a massive tartan kilt, with a huge great sporran; he had a straggly, flaming red beard that reached all the way to his tartan socks; and his fiery red hair was so wild that you could barely see his eyes through the tangle.

Benandonner felt the ground tremble as Finn drew nearer and knew that another giant was approaching. When Finn saw him and heard his mighty roar, he turned round and fled back across the Causeway, with the Scottish giant not far behind. On reaching Ireland, Finn kicked off his huge boots so he could run more easily, and one of his boots can be seen to this day, resting on the shore of Port Noffer.

He climbed the cliffs to his house, where his wife was waiting with a grand idea. "Get into the baby's pram," she said to Finn. She then put the baby's frilly blue bonnet on his head, and covered him with the baby's blankets. When Benandonner arrived, Finn was nowhere to be found and all he could see was Oonagh and an enormous baby. He turned back out across the causeway, smashing the stones as he went, so that Finn could never set foot in Scotland again.

Neither giant is alive today, but you can still see the two ends of the stepping stones; in Ireland they disappear into the sea along a stretch of coast known as the Giant's Causeway, and in Scotland they can still be seen in Fingal's Cave, on the Isle of Staffa. And if you listen really carefully, on very clear evenings, you may even be able to hear the mysterious sound of bagpipes carrying out across the sea . . . .

The Sleeping Beauty

Deep in the heart of North Wales sits a beautiful castle, which was built hundreds of years ago. A king and a queen once lived at Chirk Castle – for so it was called – and for a long time they did not have any children, and Chirk was a very quiet place. Then the Queen gave birth to a beautiful baby girl, and their magnificent castle echoed to the happy sound of the baby's laughter.

When she was a few months old, the King and Queen decided to arrange their daughter's christening and they selected all the fairies who lived nearby to be godmothers to their baby princess. They arranged a huge christening feast, to which the godmothers and their many friends were to be invited.

When the feast was over, the seven fairies, resplendent in their beautiful dresses, went up to the King and Queen, chattering and wanting to hold the baby, and full of good cheer and good wishes. Their goddaughter was to be called Isabella, and the eldest godmother asked to hold her during the christening. As she took Isabella from the arms of the King, the other godmothers began to gather round, cooing over the baby. They were very proud of their little Princess. All of a sudden, the door was thrown open with an almighty crash, and a dark, hooded figure, with long grey hair and sharp, claw-like nails, appeared in the doorway.

The King and Queen had forgotten Esmerelda – the oldest fairy of them all.

Esmerelda lived in a distant turret of the castle, and had not been seen by anyone for so many years that everyone had forgotten her. "What's going on?" she cried to the stunned guests. "Forgotten your oldest fairy, have you? Rather a mistake don't you think, especially when I have so much to offer the dear child?" Her terrifying cackle echoed throughout the hall, as the King and Queen hastily welcomed her to the christening, and beckoned her to see their daughter.

When the christening was over, it was time for the fairies to bestow their gifts upon the Princess. The first godmother laid Isabella gently in her cradle and presented her with the gift of beauty. The second godmother went up to the cradle to present the gift of good nature; the next gave good grace, and the fourth bestowed musical skills. The fifth conferred the gift of drawing, and the sixth gave the gift of a beautiful voice. The King and Queen then gave their daughter a beautiful rose bush, which they said would grow more and more beautiful with every year it bloomed. But everyone was waiting for Esmerelda's gift.

Still cackling softly to herself, the old fairy stood and pointed a long, bony finger at Isabella. "My gift is the decree that on her sixteenth birthday, your beautiful Princess will prick her finger on a spinning wheel and will die!" The guests gasped in horror and the King and Queen did not know what to do as the old fairy hobbled out, muttering curses to herself.

But everyone had forgotten the youngest fairy, who was standing quietly by the window. Blushing furiously and feeling terribly nervous, she stepped forward. "But I have not given *my* gift yet," she said hesitantly. "I cannot undo this wicked spell, but I *can* change it." She raised her magic wand over the cradle;

"She will not die –
but softly sleep
as all around
her courtiers keep
a silent guard
in slumbers deep.

Her rose will bloom
her rose will fade
one hundred times
before she's made
to stir and wake and then behold
a prince – all this I have foretold."

All the guests gathered round the youngest fairy to thank her for changing Esmerelda's spell. The King and Queen wept inconsolably for their daughter's future, hoping fervently that the horrid old fairy had been wrong.

Isabella grew up with all the beauty and skills that her godmothers had promised. She loved her home, and spent many happy hours wandering through its rooms and its terraced garden, and sitting in the kitchens with the cooks as they told her stories about life beyond Chirk. She grew up not knowing what a spinning wheel was, for the King ruled that none was to be allowed anywhere in his kingdom. This allowed him to forget about Esmerelda's curse – for how could Isabella be harmed by something that did not exist? So nobody worried as Isabella neared her sixteenth birthday . . . .

When the day finally arrived, Isabella was too excited to stay in her chambers, and went wandering around the castle until she came upon a tiny winding staircase she had never seen before. She climbed all the way up until she found herself in a room in one of the castle towers, in which stood an ancient spinning wheel. Even the King had forgotten this little room, and the only spinning wheel left in the land. "Oh, I've never seen one of these before," exclaimed Isabella to herself, "I wonder how it works." She sat at the wheel and took up the thread, but before she could begin spinning, her finger was caught by the spindle. She cried out in pain, as she sank to the floor and fell into a deep, deep sleep.

When Isabella didn't appear for her birthday party, the King organised a search party. When they finally found the young Princess, her parents realised there was nothing they could do to wake her. The King had the last spinning wheel burnt, but it was too late. He placed his daughter in the castle's state bed, and then he summoned the youngest godmother and asked if there was anything else that she could do to help them. The fairy godmother knew that all she could do was ensure that everything would be just the same for the Princess when she awoke in a hundred years. Before the King could say anything, she put the whole castle to sleep – the King and Queen and all the cooks, all the soldiers and all the animals – even the water in the castle ponds became as still as could be, and no wind was allowed to stir even the tiniest leaves on the castle trees. With one sweep of her magic wand she froze everything just as it was – and disappeared.

The years passed and the trees and bushes grew up around the castle and hid it from sight. Wild flowers covered the lawns in one great carpet, and wild roses overtook the castle gardens. Isabella's rose grew and grew, blooming more beautifully every year. Nobody passing the castle could have guessed about all the sleeping people inside.

A hundred years passed before a young prince, chasing after his runaway dog, stumbled into the castle grounds, and into a magical sleeping world. He had grown up thinking that the castle was haunted, or deserted, and there were even local tales of a princess who had been asleep inside for 100 years, but everyone had been too scared to come and find out for themselves. But the Prince could hear his dog barking inside the castle and nothing was going to stop him. He began to tear at the mass of rose briars with his sword. As he did so, the tangled briars began to draw back as if by magic, and the stunned Prince was able to walk straight up to the castle and through the castle doors into a hall filled with sleeping people!

Following the sound of his barking hound, the Prince passed the courtiers asleep on the stairs, and finally came to the state bedroom, where his dog was sitting expectantly at the end of the bed. As he put his face close to Isabella's to see if she was still breathing, her eyes opened, and everything around him began to stir and come to life once more – the spell was broken at last.

Isabella married her Prince, and they had a long and happy life at Chirk. They are, of course, long gone now, and their former home is often open to the public and bustling with the sounds of visiting families. But come the autumn, when the doors are closed to visitors and the furniture is covered up for the winter, calm falls upon the place again, and you can almost imagine that the castle and all its occupants have been put to sleep once more ....

The Three Bears

There once was a big house called Killerton, which had a little house nestling in its beautiful garden. The little house, surrounded by deep red rhododendron bushes and sweet-smelling magnolia trees, had been built as a summer house for the family who lived at Killerton. It had lattice windows, a ceiling made of straw matting and pine cones, a little chamber with a stained glass window, and a floor made from deer's knuckle bones. But as every summer ended, and the family stopped using their little house until the following spring, another family arrived from the woods nearby, a family of bears, who made the house their own . . . .

One cold, November afternoon, the little girl who lived at Killerton made her way out of her nursery, and down towards her summer house. Her mother and father had warned her not to stray too far from the big house, but she was feeling adventurous, and longed to see what became of her little house during the winter months. Maybe it was full of cobwebs and spiders, and had hedgehogs and mice living in all its nooks and crannies.

But when she arrived at the house, there were no cobwebs, and not only were there no spiders or mice, but there was a fire crackling in the grate, and there were three fresh bowls of porridge on the table, set on a crisp, clean table cloth, with steam rising from them. "Well I never," said the little girl, who had a very healthy appetite, "I'd better try some of this". So she had a little bit of porridge from the big bowl, a little bit of porridge from the middle bowl, and the porridge in the little bowl tasted so good that she couldn't stop herself, and ate it all up.

Spotting three rocking chairs by the fire, she went and sat in the largest one, but it was too hard for her and her feet didn't touch the ground. So she tried a smaller chair and it was too soft and her feet still didn't touch the ground. But the littlest chair was just right, so she sat down and began to rock backwards and forwards, until the legs suddenly snapped under her and she fell on the floor – whoever owned the chair definitely weighed less than she did.

Feeling a little bit bruised, she got up and began to look around. Inside the little chamber with the stained glass window she found three beds that hadn't been there in the summer. The biggest bed was far too lumpy, and the middle one was much too soft, but the tiniest bed was so perfect that when she lay down on it, she fell fast asleep, and dreamt of delicious, steaming porridge.

When the family of bears came home they were very surprised to find the door open and some of their porridge eaten. "Who's dipped their finger in *my* porridge?" growled Daddy Bear. "Who's had a spoonful of *my* porridge?" cried Mummy Bear. "And who's eaten all *my* porridge up?" wailed Baby Bear.

Then they noticed the chairs by the fire. "Who's been rocking in my rocking chair?" growled Daddy Bear. "Who's been messing my cushions up?" cried Mummy Bear. "And who's broken my chair *all to pieces*?" wailed Baby Bear.

So they went into the little chamber to see if they could find the naughty visitor. "Well, someone's been messing up *my* bed," said Daddy Bear. "And someone's definitely been lying on *my* bed," said Mummy Bear. "And someone's *IN* my bed" screamed Baby Bear. When the little girl heard the Baby Bear scream, she sat bolt upright and, seeing the three bears standing over her, burst into tears.

The bears, who were really very kindly, tried to stop her crying, saying that they really didn't mind that she was there. The little girl apologised through her tears for everything she had done, but explained that it really was her house sometimes too. Would they mind sharing it with her? It would be her summer house and their winter house, and she would love to visit them again in the winter if they would come and see her in the summer. The bears thought that was a lovely idea. So she stopped crying, and Mummy Bear took her by the hand and led her back up the path to Killerton, while Daddy Bear and Baby Bear waved goodbye.

Today, Killerton is open to the public, and the little house is now known as the Bear's Hut. Very few people realise just how it came by this name, or exactly what happened there all those years ago, but it would seem that the little girl and the bears got on very well, and continued to share their little summer and winter house for many years.

The Billy-Goats-Gruff

This is a story about three goats – a little brother, a middle brother, and a big brother – who lived in a place called Buckinghamshire. It was late summer, and all the grass was getting very dry due to the lack of rain, so the three Billy-Goats-Gruff – for that was their name – set off to find some fresh green grass to eat. They finally found a beautiful garden at a house called Stowe, where there was lots of water to keep all the grass fresh. "This is perfect," said the biggest Billy-Goat-Gruff, "Let's go up on to that hillside and have lunch!" So the three goats set off across the garden in a little line, each stopping to graze at any tasty-looking bits of grass on the way.

On the way to the hillside they had to cross a beautiful bridge, built over a beautiful lake, and under the bridge lived a Troll – who wasn't beautiful at all. Do you know what a Troll is? All Trolls originally come from Scandinavia, but some of the more adventurous have travelled south, and can sometimes be found in gardens and parks in other parts of Europe.

They like places that are cold and damp and dark, so often live under bridges. They can come in many different forms – large and small, fat and thin – but they are almost always VERY UGLY.

The Stowe Troll was very ugly indeed, but he had chosen to make his home at Stowe, under a very beautiful bridge, which nestled in the rare and stunning garden full of lakes and pretty buildings. This particular Troll had big, staring eyes, enormous ears and a huge nose. He was very hairy and had teeth as sharp as a shark's. He spent his days sleeping, making mud-castles in the lake and looking for food – and his very favourite food just happened to be goat.

The smallest Billy-Goat-Gruff was the first to step on to the bridge and his tiny hooves made a light tap-tap-tapping noise as he trotted across. "Who's that trotting across my bridge?" grumbled the Troll, who had been taking a nap and was always very grumpy when he was first woken up. "Oh dear," squeaked the little goat, "It's only a very little billy-goat in search of some grass to eat." "Well, I'm hungry," said the Troll, sniffing the air for the smell of goat, "And I think I might just have to gobble you up for my lunch." But the little goat was too clever for the Troll. "Oh no," he squeaked, "I think you'd better wait for my big brother – there's much more meat on him." The Troll thought for a moment. "Oh all right," he sighed, "Move on, you little pip-squeak!"

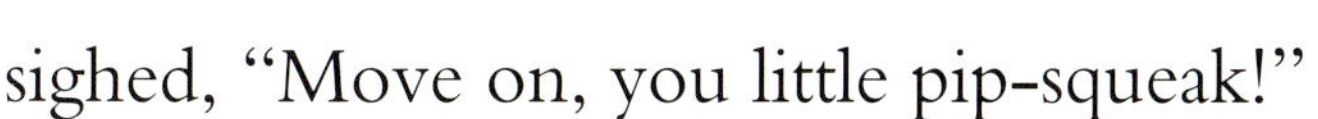

Shortly after this, the middle billy-goat came to the bridge and his big hooves made a loud tap-tap-tapping noise as he trotted across. "Who's that trotting across my bridge?" cried the Troll, who was getting hungrier and hungrier. "Oh dear," said the middle goat, "It's only a young billy-goat in search of some grass to eat." "Well, I'm ravenous," said the Troll, "And I think you're about to become my lunch." But the middle goat was too clever for the Troll. "Oh no," he said, "I think you need our big brother – he's much bigger and fatter than us." "Oh all right," sighed the Troll, licking his lips, "Be off with you."

A little while later, the biggest billy-goat came up to the bridge and his great hooves made a heavy tap-tap-tapping noise as he trotted across. "Who's that almost destroying my bridge?" roared the Troll. "It's the biggest billy-goat of all," roared the oldest billy-goat, who was used to telling his little brothers off and who wasn't going to stand for any nonsense. "Well, I'm going to have you for my lunch," boomed the Troll, as he clambered out from under the bridge. "Oh no you're not," boomed the billy-goat back, and he rushed at the head of the Troll as it appeared above the bridge, and knocked it right off with his horns. He watched as it flew up in the air and landed on the far side of the lake with a big splash.

"Time for lunch," he said as he crossed the bridge to the lush green hillside beyond. And there he joined his brothers and they all ate to their hearts' content.

HANSEL AND GRETEL

Hansel and Gretel were the children of a woodcutter who lived in a deep, wooded gorge by a river. Their mother had died when they were little, but they grew up very happily with their father, spending many hours with him, wandering through the woods and looking at all the birds, berries, mushrooms and wild flowers.

But all this was to change. Their father married again and Hansel and Gretel found themselves with a wicked stepmother who disliked children because she said they ate too much. She never gave them very much food, and they were never allowed to eat cake or sweet things. She complained and complained to the woodcutter, saying that there were just too many mouths to feed, until he gave in and agreed to take Hansel and Gretel deep into the woods so they would get lost and be unable to find their way home.

But the children were far too smart for this plan. As the woodcutter led them further and further from their cottage, Gretel laid a trail of little white pebbles behind them. When their father vanished, they were able to follow the pebbles all the way home.

The wicked stepmother was furious when they returned, and their father took them off even further into the woods. They walked so far that the children were worn out, and they finally fell asleep under a huge, old oak tree.

When they awoke the sun was setting, and their father was already miles away, but Hansel had laid a trail of breadcrumbs all the way back to their door. However, Hansel had forgotten that the wood was full of hungry birds, and the breadcrumbs had all been eaten up. The children were very hungry, and were just beginning to get scared, when they saw smoke rising above the trees a little way off, so they went in search of food and shelter.

Right in the middle of a little clearing, surrounded by a little fence, stood a sweet little cottage, painted in lots of beautiful colours. "It looks good enough to eat," said Gretel. "It *is* good enough to eat!" said Hansel, running his finger along the fence, which was made of candy sticks dusted with icing sugar. They opened the gate and went up the garden path, to find a door made of chocolate, windows made of spun sugar, and walls made of the most delicious gingerbread. No sooner had they reached the door, than a little old woman appeared and beamed at them.

"Come in, come in," she cried and the children followed her into the cottage. The old woman fed them a wonderful meal, and in the morning they had another, followed by another at lunchtime, and another in the evening.

This went on for several days, until they began to look quite plump, and Gretel started to think there was something rather strange about this little old woman.

Then one morning Hansel disappeared, and Gretel found him locked up and weeping in the hen-house. “She’s fattening us up like chickens!” cried Hansel, “She’s a wicked witch and she’s going to eat me!” “Oh no she’s not!” said Gretel very firmly, and she stormed off to the little house, where she found the old woman making a huge fire, over which to roast Hansel. “What do *you* want, little girl?” she asked Gretel. “I want you to have a look in the cellar,” said Gretel, “because I think that lots of big fat rats are living down there.” Gretel knew from her story books that witches liked to eat rats for their supper. The old woman licked her lips. “Something tasty for pudding,” she said, opening the cellar door. But before she could do anything, Gretel snatched her keys from her belt, pushed her in and locked the door.

When Gretel had let Hansel out of the hen-house, the two children had to decide what to do. Instead of just running away, Gretel decided that they should make the witch promise to be good before they let her out of the cellar. Once the little witch had changed her ways, the children loved living with her in their delicious house, and she never tried to eat them ever again. They continued to live in the gingerbread house, with lollipops and chocolate and cakes to eat. They had their father to stay as much as they liked, and they never had to live with their wicked stepmother again.

Ian Penney's Book of Fairy Tales

Ian Penney lives in Great Britain,
and so he has set his delightful illustrations
for the fairy tales included here
in houses, gardens, and estates that he has visited
throughout England, Ireland, Scotland, and Wales,
specifically those that have been preserved
by the National Trust.